AF751636

A New Life

Story by Melaina Faranda

Illustrations by Caroline Garcia

Contents

Chapter 1

A Dangerous Secret

"Firash! Where are you?"

It was his mother calling through the one window of their cramped little house. But the voice was only in Firash's head – part of the usual guilt he felt whenever he was outside, while Mother and his sisters, Leila and Aisha, were forced to stay inside two dark rooms every day. Firash tried to ignore it.

"Hurry up. We don't have all year," Abdul grumbled, readying the bat.

It was Firash's turn to bowl. He rubbed the ball against his pants to make it smoother, like the most famous bowlers did – and took a run up.

Abdul gripped a cricket bat fashioned from a piece of wood broken off a pallet. Firash bowled with a skilful spin, so that the ball sailed past on an angle. Abdul swung and missed as the ball smashed into the three uneven sticks set up as wickets.

"Yes!" Firash gave a cry of triumph as the ball rolled past and down, into a heaped mound of rubble where a building in the street had been bombed only weeks earlier.

Instantly there was a commotion as the boys all broke from their game to hunt for the ball. Firash wanted to join, but he imagined his mother calling again. She would be wanting to cook dinner, but it was too dangerous now for her or his sisters to go out onto the street to the market without being accompanied by his father. When Firash had returned from school, Mother had sent him to buy onions and a bag of rice.

The heavy sack of rice was still sitting where Firash, irresistibly drawn into the game of cricket, had propped it against the rock. But the onions had vanished.

"Has anyone seen my onions?" Firash called to the other boys, who shrugged or returned blank looks as he frantically searched, now even more worried about his mother's disappointment than a dinner without onions. He should have known better. His family had been in this town for two months – leaving food lying about here was an irresistible invitation for someone hungry. And many people in this town were hungry, some even starving.

All over the country, and for the whole time of war, there had been food shortages. Everyone knew how the army swarmed upon farming villages and helped themselves to whatever they liked: chickens, rice, vegetables, spices, dried fruits and oil – leaving far less food for farmers to trade in the town markets.

"You must never complain about these things out loud," Mother and Father had impressed on the three children. "It is too dangerous. A neighbour we drink tea and play chess with might seem to nod and express sympathy, only to report us to the authorities the next day."

It was even more difficult for Firash's sisters to hold their tongues. Being of high school age, Leila and Aisha were no longer permitted to go to school.

Almost overnight they had transformed from their usual loud and cheerful selves, full of ideas and opinions about how their country could become better, becoming sad and grim faced. They had changed from the day they tearfully returned home without their expensive schoolbooks – which had all been heaped in a pile and set on fire while the headmistress and teachers were led away by soldiers.

"It's all right for you!" Leila had once hissed at Firash, when he was attempting to scrounge some money from Mother to buy sweet pastries from the street stalls after school. "You still have your freedom." The girls were no longer able to go out into the streets to the stores or markets. If they did, they would have to be accompanied by Father and wear long flowing clothes that they weren't used to.

Being a boy, Firash still attended school, but there were many things he could not say. The only thing that relieved the strain of worrying he would say the wrong thing, anything that could bring danger to his family, was playing cricket during breaks. With cricket, Firash could forget everything that was happening, like trucks with huge tyres crushing rubble into smaller pieces as soldiers shouted and hauled people from their families and homes to be questioned.

When playing cricket, he could temporarily forget his guilt about the boys at school who gnawed on a single wizened apple for their meal. If any of his classmates were curious as to why Firash always had a full meal for lunch, no one dared ask. Especially because he did his best to share his food around. Firash knew they assumed he must have uncles who were soldiers – like Abdul, whose brother was a soldier. Abdul liked to strut about the school. He dealt out insults, and worse, that went unpunished by the teachers. Abdul was careful not to pick on Firash, however. Before Firash's arrival, he had been the star pupil. Abdul seemed curious about Firash being far ahead in his studies and obviously believed, along with the other boys, that Firash's family were in the army.

Firash almost wished they were. The reality was far worse. His family had a dangerous secret.

Chapter 2

Another Lifetime

Firash's family secret, if discovered, could see his parents branded as traitors to the new government. Not only was his mother a highly skilled translator, but she had been working undercover translating for foreign journalists reporting on what was happening here. Father was an information technology specialist who helped her with encoding messages.

Back in the capital city, which seemed almost another lifetime ago, Firash's parents had been paid foreign wages that would be considered a fortune in this small town they had fled to.

In the city, they had lived in a huge apartment, the echoing of many high-ceilinged rooms barely muffled by woven carpets and antiques polished by cleaners. Their cook prepared regular banquets for the many evenings of elaborate dinners, which were sometimes enjoyed around a long table in the Western style, and sometimes eaten cross-legged on comfortable cushions around a cloth spread on the floor, in the usual custom.

There were many lively dinner conversations with journalists, foreign aid workers and diplomats.

The conversations were loud and long in a mixture of English and their own language – about the state of the country and how it could be improved.

Firash and his sisters had attended exclusive schools for the sons and daughters of the rich, and were taught to value their country's tradition and culture while still having access to opportunities and technology. Mother often said that all people – girls and boys, men and women – should have equal opportunities.

When the war came, and those same journalists and foreign aid workers were forced to flee the country for their lives, Firash's family were left in grave danger. Each day, people were put in jail for far less cause. But David, an international documentary film-maker friend, with connections seemingly around the whole country, had arranged for them to move to this small town in the south. That's why they were living in a dingy apartment owned by the cousin of someone David had met during his travels.

Firash and his sisters were allowed to keep their first names, but Mother and Father changed theirs. Together they kept up the pretence that Father was a businessman whose import business had been damaged by international sanctions, which meant that other countries would no longer trade with the new government because of their refusal to respect human rights. Their story was that this had forced Father to shut down his business and move his family to somewhere they could live more cheaply. Mother was a housewife.

Now, as Firash removed his shoes at the door and entered the two-roomed house, Mother looked up from where she was crouched in the gloomy shadows, stirring something over a gas burner on the scuffed cement floor. It was a far different picture from when they had employed a cook and servants.

Unable to meet her eyes, Firash hefted the sack of rice into the corner of the dark room.

"Where are the onions?"

Firash bowed his head. "I lost them."

"You lost onions? How do you *lose* onions?"

Firash paused, unwilling to tell her the truth, but his mother had a way of looking at him that always made him crack. "There was a game of cricket. I put them down just for a moment. I swear it was just a moment."

Leila and Aisha looked up enviously from where they sat at a battered table, heads bent over schoolbooks Father had bought on the black market, which they were using to continue learning from Mother – whose brown eyes now flashed, as if considering punishment.

"If I had been *allowed* to go buy the onions, I would never have lost them," Aisha declared.

Then Mother sighed, and her eyes softened again into their usual warm glow. "How can I be angry at you for enjoying a moment of freedom, Firash?" she said quietly. "After all that has happened, it is a miracle that even one of my children still has it in them to play."

Chapter 3

The Trick to Lying

"The soldiers are coming back." That was the rumour swirling around the small dirt courtyard of the "school". Instead of a building with rooms, it was in an interior courtyard with crumbling walls and no ceiling. A mat was laid on the dust and the boys all sat on cushions on the mat. The teacher was grimly strict, and the lessons were dull. But Firash knew not to complain at home – he knew what his sisters would say: at least *he* was still able to go to school.

"This time they're going to search every house." Abdul puffed out his chest as he picked up the teacher's long wooden ruler and slowly pointed it around the clustered boys. "Maybe it will be my brother who finds out if your fathers are traitors."

Abdul's eyes narrowed as some of the boys flinched away from the ruler. It could be a sign that their fathers didn't support the war. Or, more likely, Firash thought, it was a simple fear that Abdul might lash out with that ruler at any time.

Abdul's eyes came to rest on Firash. Firash's heart was beating furiously in his chest as he steeled himself to meet Abdul's gaze.

"What does your father do for work?" Abdul asked. It was the first time any one of them had dared to ask.

Firash tried to keep his voice steady as he remembered the lines Father had made all the children rehearse. "He ran a business in imports, but there were sanctions and he lost money."

"Imports?"

Firash knew by now that Abdul was not only cruel – unfortunately, he was clever as well. Father and Mother had told Firash and Leila and Aisha that it was important to be honest. However, sometimes it would be necessary to lie as an act of survival. The real trick to lying was to keep things as close to the truth as possible.

"He imports hardware for computers," said Firash.

"From foreign countries!"

Firash gulped. That one couldn't be lied away. Of course it was from foreign countries – that's what importing was!

Firash nodded. Then, in the attempt to stop Abdul from going any further along this road of questioning, he made a terrible mistake.

"He imports for the army."

The other boys nodded respectfully, but Abdul looked thoughtful.

Firash knew he had to think of something quickly to distract Abdul.

"Anyway, let's go play cricket," he said. "Abdul, you can bat."

Over dinner, when the family was all seated on cushions around the mat, Firash explained what had happened at school that day. It was often this way. He and Father would now do most of the talking as Mother, Leila and Aisha peppered them with questions, hungry for any news, great or small, from the world that lay literally just beyond their door.

His mother and sisters had spent the day in a domestic drudgery of cooking and cleaning what seemed to Firash a house that could not ever be properly cleaned. It would always have oily smears and smoke stains on the ceiling, peeling paint on the walls and musty curtains with so many tears they could not all be properly mended.

Then there were their secretive lessons. Although Mother was doing her best to continue the girls' education, and especially to teach them English, she complained that for all of them it was like being in a prison with only three inmates. It was far too dangerous for Mother to communicate with her journalist friends or translate for them. Father had a phone, but had to be careful how he used it. The reception was often poor, and the internet regularly went out. There was more to be learned from the men gossiping over tea and chess or standing in small frowning huddles out on the street. It was Father and Firash alone who were able to bring updates into the house.

"You told him that Father imported computer hardware for the army?" Mother repeated.

Firash nodded, unhappily aware of the worried glances being exchanged between his parents.

"And this boy?" Father asked with a frown. "Is he likely to say anything to anyone? To make trouble?"

Firash contemplated the way Abdul tormented the others. Abdul had steered clear of him until now. Perhaps because of Firash's more expensive clothes and city accent, Abdul must have thought they were connected to the army. But if he mentioned Firash's father to his brother, Firash's claim could be easily checked. And they might discover Father wasn't even using his real name.

Firash nodded.

Now his parents looked alarmed.

"We have to leave," Mother urged.

Father threw his arms up. "And go to where? Surely, it's going to look worse if we suddenly leave overnight. And with the army nearby – we can't take the risk."

Tears glistened in Mother's dark eyes. "Gul," she said gently. "We've seen this happen to our dearest friends. I am not going to leave our children orphans."

Mother turned suddenly to Firash, Leila and Aisha. "We've taught you that all people should be given equal opportunities. For you girls, this is no kind of life without education. And for you, too, Firash. We don't want you to be conscripted into the army. But to flee will involve great risk. And if we make it, we will have to live in a new country. Perhaps never return here. I know you are young, but your opinions are important, and I am going to ask you what it is you wish for."

Leila and Aisha didn't hesitate. "We want to go to school."

Mother nodded. "Firash?"

Firash glanced at his sisters, and at the new worry lines creasing his parents' foreheads. He thought about school, which he was fortunate enough to attend just because he was a boy. While there were boys like Abdul who grew up to become soldiers, there would never be peace. "I want to leave, too."

Father sighed. "I'll try to send an encrypted message to our friends."

Chapter 4

A Secret Plan

Father managed to get in touch with their film-making friend, David – the one who had found this house for them.

David was able to contact some other friends of theirs, who had their own contacts. Eventually, it was arranged for them to get a lift from another town where, in turn, they would be taken to someone who would guide them through the mountains. They were to cross the mountains to reach the border under the cover of night. Flashlights would be easily spotted by soldiers on patrol, so they would need to wait for a night when the moon was at least half full to light their journey through the mountains.

Firash only knew this because, through the thin curtain that divided their beds, he overheard his parents whispering at night.

"We cannot let the children know the details," Mother said. "It is too big a responsibility for them to keep secret. They might accidentally give our plans away."

"Or worse," Father added. "We don't want them being questioned by the soldiers."

With this, Firash felt doubly terrible about the lie he had blurted to Abdul. The same lie that was prompting this terrifying risk his family was about to take. If they were caught, his parents might be taken away and he might never see them again. He and his sisters might be separated, only to go hungry on the streets. The children of “traitors” were not treated well.

Knowing this, he had hardly been able to focus while at school. The one relief was still playing cricket at break time. Abdul seemed more friendly than before, but there was a slyness in his smile Firash didn’t trust. Everyone knew the soldiers would be coming any day now. It was an open secret how people had already started to hide food and other stores, hoping desperately to be spared having their houses stripped of everything.

Firash made sure to bowl in a way that Abdul could easily hit sixes straight off. He deliberately got some of his spelling wrong so that Abdul would have the most correct answers. And when he caught Abdul eyeing a handful of plump dates Mother had packed in his lunch, Firash quickly offered to share.

At home, Mother had sewed deep inside pockets into the long robes she and the girls had to wear in public. They were for carrying their jewellery and other small items of sentiment. "We must not be seen to be carrying too much," she cautioned. "It needs to look as if we are visiting 'Auntie' for a day only." They would board a bus as a family, Father said, and the story, if asked, was that they were all going to visit an ailing elderly aunt. They were bringing her treats and specialties from their southern town.

They had already been forced to give so much away when leaving their city home, but they could not be seen to be carrying packs or bags without arousing suspicion or questions.

Yet, although clearly anxious, Mother and Leila and Aisha were laughing more. They no longer slumped at the table. They were each energised by the prospect of escaping to a better life.

On the day before they were to catch the bus, Firash was barely able to keep still during his lessons at school.

Abdul approached him at the cricket game during their break. He scrutinised Firash. "I told my family about you."

Firash's heart thudded. His fists clenched around the cricket ball.

"My mother said you should come back to my place one afternoon." Abdul walked back towards the game.

Firash felt as if he would slump to the ground in relief, even as Abdul turned and added, "But not to play cricket – you're terrible at it. Tomorrow?"

Firash managed to shake his head. "We have to visit my auntie. But the day after would be good." That was the secret of lying, to stick as close to the truth as possible – the day after was good only because he would be far away from Abdul and this town.

Chapter 5

Escape

They boarded the bus, with Mother and the girls being shepherded by Father, while Firash carried a basket full of "food" to gift to their sick auntie.

The bus was packed with women, accompanied by male relatives, bringing scanty harvests to or from markets. A few carried chickens that occasionally clucked and the aisle of the bus was filled with sacks of rice.

Outside was harsh and dusty, barren of grass or trees, and with stark stony mountains looming in the distance. Through the occasional village twisted a river with a fringe of green on either side where people irrigated their crops.

Periodically, the bus stopped to let people on or off, or slowed to skirt around a crater where a bomb had exploded.

At a checkpoint, Firash felt his father stiffen beside him as soldiers boarded the bus.

"Identity cards!" they demanded as they made their way heavily down the bus aisle, kicking aside cloth bundles and sacks. "Show us your identity cards!"

Amongst the general scrabbling for the cards, Father reached into his vest pocket and calmly waved his in front of a soldier.

"Where are you going to?" the soldier demanded.

Father named the town and added, "We are going to visit my aunt."

The soldier gave a broad smile. "My cousin lives there. Do you know Mohammad the spice seller? Everyone in town knows him."

Firash watched, heart in mouth, as Father decided the best course of action: whether to bluff and pretend he did or state plainly that he didn't. Father chose the latter. "I am sorry, I don't believe I have met him. I can ask my aunt?"

The soldier regarded him shrewdly before curtly nodding and kicking a bag of rice aside to stomp towards passengers further along the aisle. Firash realised that it had been a trick question – there had been no cousin or spice seller. The soldier had been testing to see if Father really knew the town and Father had narrowly avoiding falling into a trap.

The bus was on its way again. The land beyond seemed one endless stretching plain of sand and dust with the distant mountains slowly looming closer.

Except for the stark jagged range beyond, the town the bus rumbled into looked much the same as the one they had just left. There were the usual squares filled with rubble and broken slabs of cement where buildings had been.

They were met by a man lounging against a blue car that was covered in dents and scrapes. "I will take you to visit your aunt," he said loudly, for the benefit of others milling around the bus.

Firash squished into the back seat with Mother, Leila and Aisha. The car's upholstery was cracked and torn, and the window handles were broken. It was entirely unlike the sleek black SUV they had owned in the city, in which their driver, Ali, would drop Firash and the girls at school each day.

A long narrow cloud of dust plumed behind them as the car sped away and jerked and grumbled along a dirt road leading to the foothills.

"We are here," the driver announced after a while.

A giant mountain with fierce cliffs and crags dwarfed a small stark shelter at its base with walls the colour of the surrounding hills. Outside the shadowed doorway, two tethered goats bleated as a girl bearing two jugs slipped past, on her way to fetch water from a hand pump around the side of the building.

Firash watched, dazed by the strangeness of this place, as a man wearing a black turban emerged from the building, his arms crossed against his chest. Grim faced, he spoke some terse words with the driver, then turned to Father.

Father stepped forward only to engage in an intense conversation with the man. Both shook their heads and waved their arms about until, finally, they leant closer to hook their index fingers and show they had reached agreement.

Father stepped back and slipped his hand into one of the pockets in his vest.

At the sight of the wad of money Father drew out, the man broke into a sudden grin revealing many gaps where teeth had been. "Welcome to my home," he said cheerfully. "I am Halim." He gestured to Mother and the girls. "Your wife and daughters should come inside and meet my own wife and daughters."

They would be given a meal before it grew dark, then they would wait until it was night and the moon was up. Halim said it would be safer to lead them across the border at night.

Halim's wife took the meal to her husband and Father. She obviously considered Firash still a child, as he ate in a room with the women and children. Sick with excited fear, he did not want to offend his hosts, but could barely eat the dumplings pressed upon him. They had been warned that the mountains were patrolled by bands of soldiers. It was difficult to know who could be bribed or who would arrest them. But the aim was not to be seen or caught in the first place.

Chapter 6

Crossing the Border

Firash was shaken awake from where he lay slumped against a wall. "It's time to go," Mother whispered. Leila and Aisha were also yawning as they sleepily rose to be served strong sweet tea by Halim's wife. Halim paced by the door, clearly anxious to depart.

Firash shivered. It was a freezing desert night and they had not been able to bring any more than their usual coats and scarves, for fear of rousing suspicion.

His eyes slowly adjusted to the dim light cast by a half moon. As they wound along what might have been a goat path, the sound of their shoes crunching across dry stony ground seemed deafening. No one dared speak, as their breaths puffed out in icy clouds.

In the daytime, the mountain had seemed high enough. Now, at night, with every step they took, it got steeper. Surely it was impossible that they would be able to get to the other side before sunrise.

Suddenly, from one of the slopes came a shout. Then a flash and boom.

"Down!" their guide hissed.

Firash dived to the ground instantly, crawling on his belly to get himself closer to Aisha, who had fallen heavily to the ground.

Aisha whimpered with pain. "I've hurt my foot," she murmured to Firash. "I think I twisted my ankle. If they come closer, you'll have to leave me behind."

Firash gulped. He did not want to think about the consequences for his parents if they were caught. Instead, he whispered fiercely, "We would never do that!"

There was another boom. A commotion of confused shouts. Then stillness.

Eventually, from the silence, Halim beckoned. He gestured for them to follow him in a crawl around the slope into the shadowy cover of a ravine. "We will have to go along a different path," he said quietly.

Aisha was unable to stand on her twisted ankle without crying out in pain. Mother bound it tightly with her headscarf, then Father and Firash supported her from either side as she limped between them. It was going to cause considerable delay, and Halim made his frustration clear by refusing to slow his pace.

Firash had not known that it was possible to stop feeling any weariness or exhaustion, simply through having a body electric with fear. The whole walk felt like an endless journey through a nightmare from which there would be no waking.

Finally, however, they reached the pass from which they could see down into the plains beyond.

Halim indicated the path that wound down the mountain. "I will leave you here. I must return before daybreak." He pointed to the silvery moonlit shadow of what looked like a dried-up riverbed snaking into the distance below. "That is the border. When you cross the river, walk to the east towards three large rocks. A truck will come to pick you up."

Firash felt his whole family's tension, once their guide had taken his leave. It was as if they could not descend the mountain soon enough. But with having to support Aisha, the trudge to the riverbank dragged on. Until suddenly, they were stumbling across the stony pebbles and dirt of the dried-up watercourse, and on the other side.

As the sun rose, they leant against the three rocks, thawing their icy fingers.

Leila broke the exhausted silence. "Do you think the driver will come?" she asked, voicing what everyone had been secretly thinking, but had not dared to say aloud. "The road looks barely used. It's hardly even a track."

"Don't be foolish, Leila," Father said. "Of course he will come. Where there is money to be made, people will leap at the chance."

Firash was not so sure, as he surveyed the deserted plain stretching out before them. It felt so barren and empty. What if his parents had been lied to or tricked by Halim? They themselves had warned the children that in hard times people could do dishonest things. What if Halim had just taken Father's money without any intention of arranging a truck to meet them here on the other side of their country's border?

Even after what Father had said to Leila, Firash could see from his parents' frowns that they were possibly worrying about the same thing. Especially when, as Mother carefully shared out dates, nuts and the bottles of water they'd refilled back at Halim's home, she said, "Don't eat or drink everything at once. We might need to make them last a while."

"It's here!" Firash shouted, spotting a white billowing approaching from the distance.

A truck trundled into view, kicking up clouds of dust.

The driver addressed Father, who nodded and handed over another thick wad of money from his other vest pocket before the driver ushered them in.

Father was to be seated in the front. Mother, the girls and Firash were to sit in the tray amongst, of all things, sacks of onions.

It would be a long and tiring journey to this country's capital, where their visas had been arranged for them by contacts of Mother and Father's film-maker friend, David. He had also sent through enough money to purchase plane tickets to a new country and a new life ...

Chapter 7

Beginning

"Maybe I could start next week?" Firash looked nervously at his reflection in the mirror, as his mother gave a last tug to straighten his shirt.

She shook her head. "It's important you all start school as soon as possible. There is so much missed time to make up for, especially for the girls. But you, too, Firash – you will need to improve your English, especially reading and writing. And Father and I need to spend the days looking for jobs."

In the kitchen of the apartment, Leila and Aisha were almost bursting with excitement in their new school clothes. Each wore a headscarf over her newly washed hair.

It had been a long journey, and the process of applying to settle in this new country had been complicated, with long waiting periods. But they were finally here, in this new small apartment in a new city on the other side of the world.

Leila and Aisha were thrilled with their new life. On the weekend they had gone for a walk as a family to the park and had eaten ice cream. It had felt strange to be in a place with so many green trees.

The roads had no potholes and there were so many brand-new buildings with no bombing or brick rubble in sight. It was odd not to fear that soldiers might come around the corner. Children ran around kicking balls, while the adults chatted under shelters around tables laden with food.

"People here have so much to eat!" Firash had commented to his sisters. "It's like there are never any shortages."

Despite Mother always eating less so that the children and Father could have more, by the time they had fled their country, they were all used to times of being hungry. Before they found this apartment, they had stayed for a time with the family's film-maker friend, David.

At David's place, where he lived with his daughter, there was a small room called a pantry with shelves jostling with tins and jars. There was an enormous fridge, with food stuffed onto the shelves, and a freezer compartment that made ice and held frozen foods. After their time in the village, it seemed impossible that all that food could ever be eaten by a family of only two people!

In every moment there were new wonders. Back home, the war had been going on for so long that Firash could barely remember his city before the bombs and collapsed buildings. Here, many of the houses and buildings were new, with huge shopping centres that, unlike the street stalls and markets in the village back home, were teeming with shops that sold many versions of the same thing. It made Firash dizzy to look at them.

Even if he'd had the money to buy anything, how would he choose? And there was no bargaining here either. Prices were written on stickers, or barcodes flashed prices up on screens, and that was the final word.

People walked as if they were unafraid, and women walked freely without having to be accompanied by men.

Still, there were things Firash missed. Playing cricket and flying kites with the other boys, the stirring call to prayer that punctuated each day. The aromatic smells of street food.

And school. Even though his old school had been small, and was largely ruled by the nasty Abdul, Firash had been known and liked there. He had seemed to fit in.

Chapter 8

First Day at School

"Welcome to our school, Firash. We know you've had a big journey to get here. We're happy that you're going to be one of our students, and hope you appreciate all the wonderful opportunities our school can offer." Mrs Kentish, the school principal, seemed genuinely excited about Firash being there as she and Mother accompanied him to his classroom.

At the door, Firash gulped. Through the window in the door, he could see colourful pictures and posters all over the wall. There were lots of chairs and desks. It was almost the opposite to his school back home, which had had plain brick walls and no roof, only cloudless blue sky. There they had sat on cushions on a mat while the teacher stood in front of a blackboard.

Mother enveloped him in a big hug. "You will be fine," she whispered. "I know it."

Firash smiled bravely, but he felt so alone. Although the primary and high school shared a playground, Leila and Aisha were in the high school and would have different break times. He wouldn't know anyone.

You can do this, he told himself. *You climbed a mountain in the dark to get here. You half carried your sister. This should be easy!* But he wanted only to hide as he watched the curious expressions of the class. His new teacher, Ms Lee, announced in a bright, cheerful voice, "Class, this is our new student, Firash. He has come from a very long way away and I hope that all of you will make him feel welcome. Sam, I'd like you to be Firash's buddy this week, please, and show him around the school."

"Hey, Firash." A boy with a floppy blond fringe acknowledged him, but Firash saw that it was without enthusiasm.

Ms Lee gestured to the empty desk beside Sam. "Firash, this will be your seat for now."

Firash sat and tried to concentrate. Mother had practised English with the children often, but now it seemed as if everyone spoke so quickly and with accents Firash wasn't used to, which made it tricky for him to pick out words.

He was surprised when some of the children called out and Ms Lee did not seem to get angry. Back at home, anyone calling out without being directly addressed by the teacher would have been in big trouble.

When break time came, Sam showed Firash where the toilets and canteen were, but when some other boys passed by with a cricket bat and ball, Sam ran off to join them.

Firash stood shuffling his feet, eyes downcast, not wanting people to look at him and see how alone he was.

A couple of girls broke away from a huddle of students.

"I'm Ava," the tall blonde one said, introducing herself.

"And I'm Evie," the smaller curly-haired girl said.

Firash nodded and gave a shy smile. "Please speak slowly? My English is not good."

"Where are you from?"

When Firash told them, they both looked blank, as if they had never heard of his country.

"You can come and eat with us," Ava said.

Firash nodded gratefully and went to sit with the group. Most of them had lunch boxes filled with strange new foods he'd only just become aware of since arriving in the country. One had sushi, another a salad. Two had sandwiches.

Firash opened the container Mother had packed, and the girls were clearly fascinated to see rice and curry and how he scooped it up with torn bits of flatbread.

"Your lunch looks good," Ava said.

Firash instantly offered her the container. Back home, hospitality was important. If someone expressed admiration for something, you gave it to them.

Ava smiled and shook her head.

"Please have some?" Firash said.

"Um, no, thanks."

"No, you must have some," Firash insisted. This was how it was in his country. You must offer three times.

Ava looked embarrassed. "I have already eaten."

Firash felt confused. It was only on her third refusal that he realised she really didn't want any of his lunch.

"What are the schools like where you come from?" Evie asked.

Firash considered. With his limited English, how much could he tell them? Should he tell them that he had only ever gone to school with boys, and that girls went to different schools and were not allowed to go to high school? Could he tell them about Leila and Aisha and the day the soldiers had gone to their school and marched the teachers away? How could he explain that at school, they sat on cushions and listened to the teacher and didn't do what Ms Lee called "group work" at different tables? Or how at his last school, there were no posters or computers, and few books, and no roof either, only the open sky?

"School is not the same," he said finally. "It is better here."

The girls nodded, satisfied, but Firash felt the ache of his difference. These girls with their shiny hair and kind smiles and talk of going to the beach on the weekend, they would never be able to understand how it was to come from a place where girls had to stay inside, and where the streets were not safe for anyone.

Chapter 9

A Caged Lion

"How was your first day?" Mother asked over their meal.

Leila and Aisha clamoured to tell their stories.

"I will be learning French," Aisha said. "And biology."

"And my class is doing art," Leila said. "You should see – there is a whole room full of paints and brushes."

"There are computers in every room, too!" Aisha said, adding, "And boys and girls sit together."

"One boy asked about my headscarf," Leila said.

"And what did you tell them?" Father asked.

Leila shrugged. "I said it was our religion and we choose to wear it out of respect when we're outside the house. But I didn't get to say much more, because some other students said that it was up to all girls and women to choose for ourselves what we believe and want to wear, and not be judged by others."

"And what about you, Firash?" asked Mother.

Firash shrugged. "It was all right."

Father frowned and seemed to be about to say something, but Mother shook her head in quick warning. "When something is very new, even if it is good, it can sometimes be hard to appreciate until we feel more familiar with it," she said.

Firash nodded, wanting only to stop being the focus of his family's attention. It was different for Leila and Aisha – they had spent months cooped up at home. For them, this new life could only seem like a paradise. But for Firash, even though there had been the war, he had still had his freedom. He had had friends, both in the city then in the town they had moved to. He had been able to play cricket every day. In many ways he had become a hero for Mother, going to buy and fetch everything she needed that she was unable to get for herself when Father was out.

Firash knew he should be happy to be here in this new country. A country where not only he but also his sisters would have opportunities. A country where they would not go hungry, or risk being taken by soldiers. A country where hopefully at some stage he would stop having the regular nightmares of their escape through that mountain range as they had crossed the border. It had been strange and dizzying to listen to Ava and Evie and their friends talking at lunchtime. Even when he could pick up on their English, the things they cared and complained about seemed so strange to him.

And back at their apartment, he felt like a caged lion. There were no other boys he knew to go and fly kites or play cricket with. No tea seller to grin a toothless grin or chide the boys as they careened around. Perhaps this was how his mother and sisters had felt back at home – like caged lionesses, unable to move about freely through the streets?

He knew he should not and could not complain. They were lucky to have escaped with their lives. Lucky that there was an abundance of food and always a shop just around the corner to get more. So why did he feel so flat and empty?

Chapter 10

Coming Home

For the rest of the week, Ms Lee didn't seem to realise that Sam was only pretending to be Firash's buddy, then running off to join the other kids on the sports field the moment they left the classroom. Firash did not feel brave enough to tell Sam that he would like to play sport with them.

Instead, he wandered over to join Ava and Evie and their other friends. Although they had adopted Firash into their group, he felt strange and self-conscious under the fire of constant questions. What was it like where he came from? What did people wear? What music did they listen to? What kind of movies did they watch?

He knew they were only being friendly, and they were helpful when it was Firash's turn to ask a question about a new word or an explanation for how something worked. Yet he still felt unable to answer all their questions with his limited English.

Instead, he found himself glancing over to the field where some of the boys in his class would be playing a game of football or bouncing balls on the basketball court. Most of all he felt a pang of envy when they played cricket. He would have loved to join in, but felt too shy.

"We'll get you reading and writing in English in no time!" Ms Lee was kind and patient, as was the teaching assistant, but any special attention made Firash feel as if he was standing out.

At home, he listened to his sisters recount their days – what they had learned and the girls they had made friends with. Firash stayed silent about his own day, preferring to read the practice books Ms Lee gave him each day to take home to read at night.

Father had found work in a biscuit factory. Each evening, although he smiled to hear the girls interrupt each other to share their stories, his shoulders slumped, and his face was weary.

Firash had overheard Mother say to Father, "But the pay is so little. Back home you were high up in information technology. You have a university degree. How is it that they do not see this, but have you stand on an assembly line making biscuits?"

"Hush, my dear. Those days have changed. For now, this is our way forward. We always knew that we would do what was necessary for our children's futures, to raise them in a place of peace."

Mother was silent, then said, "As we both chose this, I will try harder to find work, too."

And only days later, Mother made an announcement. "I have found work! I'll be translating for women in a migrant centre." She turned and spoke tenderly to Firash. "I will still be home for you in the mornings. But in the afternoons, you will all have to get the school bus home."

With his whole family seeming now to be so busy and getting on with their new lives, Firash felt as if he were being left behind.

"Is everything okay?"

Firash looked up.

Ava's face was creased with concern.

"Yes," he said. "Everything is okay. Why?"

Ava smiled. "You didn't answer my question from before."

"I am sorry. What did you ask?"

"I asked if you want to go play out on the sports field. You're always looking over there. Why don't you go join in?"

Firash shifted uncomfortably. He didn't know how to tell her that he felt too shy. What if the other boys didn't want him joining in?

But Ava took matters into her own hands. "Come on," she ordered Firash. "Follow me."

Firash trailed after Ava onto the sports field and over to where a group of kids were playing cricket.

"Can we play, too?" Ava asked.

"Only if you're fielders," Sam said.

Ava rolled her eyes. "Okay. But we get to have a turn at bowling and batting, too."

Firash stood out on the lushly watered sunlit grass and waited for some action to come his way. When the ball was eventually hit in his direction, he launched into the air and caught it. There was a cheer from the fielders, then another cheer when he did it again a bit later.

When it was Firash's turn to bowl, Sam was batting. Nobody had been able to get him out. Firash felt the familiar thrill of being back in the game as he rubbed the ball against his pants. It didn't matter where he was – a square cleared from the rubble surrounded by the honking of trucks and smell of cooking fires, or this neat green field fringed by big trees. Finally, this was something that he knew and loved. When he played cricket, it felt so familiar, as if deep inside, some part of him was coming home.

He took a run up and bowled.

Sam hit the ball with a thwack and ran between the wickets before readying for the next ball.

Firash took another run up, this time spinning the ball as he hurled it so that it went sailing past Sam's upturned bat and smashed into the wickets.

"Yes!" Ava shouted.

Firash smiled, especially when he saw Sam's expression of shock transform into something that looked a lot like grudging admiration.

The lunch bell rang. As they walked back into class, Sam said to Firash, "Do you want to play cricket with us at lunchtime tomorrow?"

For the first time since they had arrived in this country, Firash felt he was able to show others something he was good at. Perhaps – as they were for his mother and sisters – things here could be good for him, too.

He raised his head and flashed Sam a smile. "I would like that."